This is Hen. This is Fox.

The hen shed is big.

It is on top of the fox den.

Hen is huffing and puffing.
She has a bun.

Fox sits and thinks.

"No hen sings as well as you!"
grins Fox.

"Sing to me!" Fox begs.

Hen sings a song to Fox.

As she sings, Hen lets go of
the bun.

The bun drops off the shed.

Dash! Fox is so quick.
He gets the bun!

This is Hen. This is Fox.